MOON, GORGEOUS MOON

M.H. Bradford

An Ivory Dog Press LLC Book

MOON, GORGEOUS MOON by M.H. Bradford
Published by Ivory Dog Press LLC
www.ivorydogpressllc.com

Conceived, written, and formatted by M.H. Bradford
www.mhbradford.com

Illustrated by Koraljka

ISBN: 978-0692985694

For Laura, because this wouldn't be possible without her

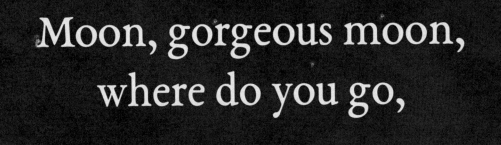

Moon, gorgeous moon,
where do you go,

When your light starts to fade
and you fall down below?

Do you swim with the fishes
beneath the blue sea,

Beside stingrays, dolphins, and in schools more than three?

Is it treasure that you seek
from ships we once knew,

In the darkest of depths
of the vast open blue?

Perhaps you dig deep
right under our feet,

In caves full of creatures
we have yet to meet.

To light up their way
through the darkest of dark,

For no one knows but you, moon,
the adventures in which they embark!

Do you
sink
beneath the
canopy of
evergreens
so tall,

To dance
with
lightning
bugs and
animals
that crawl?

To protect them as they bathe
in your sweet gentle light,

Or is it you they protect
on the stormiest of nights?

Or maybe, just maybe,
you disappear,

For others to see
who aren't so near.

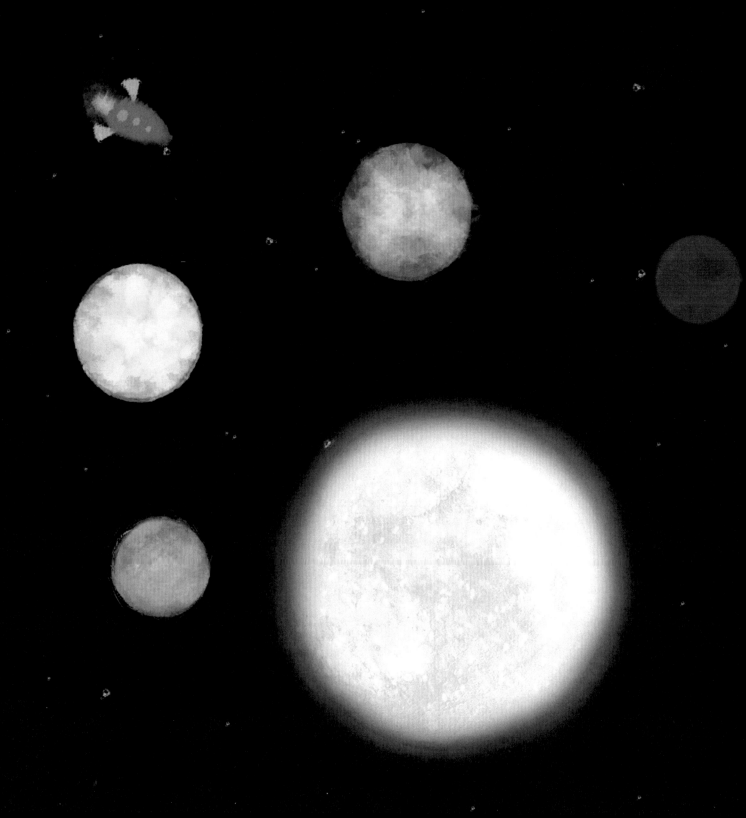

But wherever you go,
moon, gorgeous moon...

...I know you'll be back
tomorrow, so soon.

M.H. Bradford is a native of Roanoke, Virginia, where he lives with his wife Laura, their son, Sam, and a sweet golden retriever, Willow. Previously a Respiratory Care Practitioner, he is currently a professional stay-at-home dad. Inspired by Sam's wonder, blooming imagination, and love—and with his wife's support—he began his adventure writing children's books. MOON, GORGEOUS MOON is his debut.

73910885R00015

Made in the USA
Lexington, KY
12 December 2017